Have fun finding Nat in all the special places on Nantucket!

Cheryl S. Bar

Where's Nat?

A Nat, Nat, The Nantucket Cat Adventure

Written by **Peter W. Barnes** *and* Cheryl Shaw Barnes

Illustrated by **Susan Arciero**

Order our books through your local bookstore or book website by title, or by calling **1-800-441-1949** or from our website at **www.VSPBooks.com**.

For a brochure, ordering information and author school visit information, e-mail us or write to:

VSP Books
P.O. Box 17011
Alexandria, VA 22302
mail@VSPBooks.com

ISBN 978-1-893622-19-7

Library of Congress Catalog Card Number: 2007928265

10 9 8 7 6 5 4 3 2 1

Printed in the United States of America

**Find Nat hidden in each illustration,
along with all of the items in the borders.**

To our Nantucket family and friends, including our parents, Curtis and Joan Barnes (Dad is the Town Crier and appears on the Christmas Stroll page); our brother, Tom, and our nieces, CeCe and Audrey; David, Mandy, little David, and Jay Kiernan; Bryan, Anne, and Madeleine Jacoboski, and our neighbor, Alfred Bernard.

--P.W.B. and C.S.B.

For help and assistance in completing this book, we wish to acknowledge Chuck Gifford of Nantucket Cottage Hospital and Jim Lentowski of the Nantucket Conservation Foundation. Thanks to Catherine Howell back in Virginia for her edits, comments, and suggestions.

A special thanks to our daughter, Maggie Jerde, who came up with the idea!

--P.W.B and C.S.B.

For Brooke Elizabeth

--S.A.

Nat, Nat, the Nantucket Cat, welcomes one and all,
At the Steamboat Wharf, in summer, winter, spring, and fall!
"Watch your step and get your bags!" our furry friend meowed.
Find Nat waiting for you, hiding somewhere in the crowd!

Nantucket's many festivals are big and fun and grand.
(To Islanders, they rank among the finest in the land!)
Nantucket honors daffodils each spring with a parade.
The antique cars on Main Street make a splendid promenade!

Lightship baskets, ice cream cones, and candy, cakes and breads,
Flowers, postcards, puzzles, T-shirts, books, Nantucket Reds,
Kites and toys and bathing suits and flip-flops for your feet,
Benches, bricks, and cobblestones—you'll find them all on Main Street!

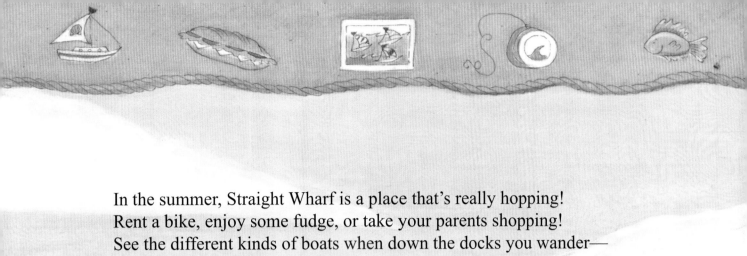

In the summer, Straight Wharf is a place that's really hopping!
Rent a bike, enjoy some fudge, or take your parents shopping!
See the different kinds of boats when down the docks you wander—
Motorboats and sailboats—there's a big one over yonder!

Nat loves going to the beach, to play and get some sun.
He'll sometimes build a sandcastle, to have a little fun.
Or maybe build a MOUSE of sand—that Nat's a clever fella!
Don't forget your towel and bucket, shovel and umbrella.

At the island's Whaling Museum, you'll hear a lot of tales
Of ships and captains and their crews who searched the seas for whales.
Nat is here exploring, but he might end up in peril!
If he doesn't watch it, he could fall into a barrel!

Sailing, sailing, faster, faster, over the ocean blue,
In a sailboat or a whaleboat—any boat will do!
The voyage gets exciting when some whales come up to play.
It's even more exciting when they blow "hello" your way!

Nantucket's Atheneum holds some favorite books of Nat's,
Including ones of mice and men and ones of cats in hats!
Sometimes, there is a book fair on the lawn right next to Weezie—
That's what they call the kids' library—come and read! It's easy!

The fireworks on Jetties Beach on Independence Day
For many is the summer's most spectacular display.
Look up! Is it a bird, a plane, or could it be a star?
No, it's our favorite kitty, twinkle, twinkle from afar!

Support the Cottage Hospital by taking in a show,
A picnic on the beach, along with everyone you know!

Nat is quite accomplished at these instrumental things—
Look closely and you might observe him somewhere in the strings!

Almost just as famous as Nantucket's frequent fogs
Are Nantucket cranberries, grown in their famous bogs!
The Cranberry Festival harvest is a favorite every fall—
Fill your basket quickly now, or Nat might get them all!

Each winter, there's a visitor who joins the Christmas Stroll—
That jolly elf named Santa Claus, direct from the North Pole!
When Nat sees Santa coming, he becomes so effervescent!
He knows that Santa never fails to bring a catnip present!

The steamship heads around Brant Point to take us home again.
From the deck, we'll wave good-bye, toss pennies in, and then,
Give thanks for our Nantucket times, and each of us will pray,
That to this very special place we'll all return one day…

Notes for Parents and Teachers
About Special Places and Events on Nantucket

Where's Nat? A Nat, Nat, the Nantucket Cat Adventure features many of the special places and events on Nantucket.

The book begins with a busy arrival scene at the town **Steamboat Wharf**, where ferryboats operated by the Steamship Authority carry people, cars, and trucks to and from the island year-round.

The **Daffodil Festival** is held the last weekend of April to celebrate the end of winter. More than three million daffodils bloom in Nantucket from early April to mid-May. The highlight of the weekend is the Annual Antique Car Parade, which features more than 100 daffodil-decorated antique vehicles.

When spring turns to summer, the sidewalks of **Main Street** become crowded with seasonal visitors patronizing shops, galleries, and restaurants.

At the bottom of Main Street, the shopping, browsing, and dining continue on **Straight Wharf**, where many motorboats and sailboats dock for the season. The Hy-Line ferryboats arrive and depart from this wharf.

The island is home to many wonderful beaches. A popular and convenient one for summer visitors is **Jetties Beach**, named after the man-made stone pilings that protect the entrance of the harbor and prevent sand from flowing into the ship channel. In August, the beach is the site of the Annual Sandcastle and Sculpture Day.

Nantucket's whaling heritage is on display at the Nantucket Historical Association's **Whaling Museum** on Broad Street. Among the exhibits, as depicted in the illustration, is a 46-foot-long skeleton of a sperm whale that washed ashore on New Year's Day 1998.

Living whales can still be seen southeast of Nantucket in the Great South Channel. Along with whale watching, island **water activities** include swimming, fishing, boating, sailing, surfing, windsurfing, kayaking, and canoeing.

The **Atheneum** on lower India Street is home to many wonderful and historic book collections, including one for children in the Weezie Library. Book sales and other activities are held on the library lawn.

Jetties Beach is a great place to watch the annual **Fourth of July fireworks**.

Jetties Beach is also the site of the annual **Boston Pops on Nantucket** concert in August. The event raises funds for the Nantucket Cottage Hospital.

There are many fun, interesting activities on Nantucket in the "off season," including the **Cranberry Festival** held by the Nantucket Conservation Foundation each fall. The foundation maintains the island's cranberry bogs and many other properties and natural habitats.

The first weekend in December is the **Christmas Stroll**, part of Nantucket Noel, a month-long celebration organized by the Nantucket Island Chamber of Commerce.